For Oliver Sherwood – GS

For Lauren and Dan – RR

First published 2009 by Macmillan Children's Books
a division of Macmillan Publishers Limited
20 New Wharf Road, London N1 9RR
Basingstoke and Oxford
Associated companies throughout the world
www.panmacmillan.com

ISBN: 978-0-230-71223-2 (HB)
ISBN: 978-0-230-73633-7 (PB)

1 3 5 7 9 8 6 4 2
A CIP catalogue record for this book is available from the British Library.
Printed in Belgium by Proost

Gillian Shields

Henry's Holiday

Illustrated by Rosie Reeve

MACMILLAN CHILDREN'S BOOKS

There was snow everywhere, white and smooth and slippery. All the baby penguins were having fun, sliding on the ice and diving into the water.

"Come and play, Henry!" they shouted.

But Henry didn't want to play.
He was too cold.

"If you go and play you'll soon get warm," said Mummy
Penguin, wrapping a scarf round him and giving him a kiss.
Henry waddled slowly across the ice to the water's edge.

"Dive in, Henry!" said his friend Splash the seal. "Come and play!"
Very, very carefully, Henry stretched out his foot and tested the water.

"Ooooh," he gasped. "It's freezing!" Henry waddled all
the way back to Mummy Penguin, very, very quickly.

Henry put on his hat.
But he was still cold.

He put on his fluffy waistcoat.
But he was still cold.

He put on his big furry boots.
But he was still cold.

"I'm so tired of the snow,"
sighed Henry.

Henry began to dream about sandy beaches and
palm trees. He dreamed about coconuts and pineapples
and gorgeous yellow sunshine.

He decided to build his very own
tropical island, all made of snow.

The other baby penguins had great fun playing on the snow island.

But it was no use. Henry was still sh-sh-shivery cold.
"I need a holiday," he said. "A very hot holiday."

One day, a boat came close to the ice.
Henry could not believe his luck.

He jumped on board. "Goodbye snow!"
Henry laughed. "Goodbye, baby penguins."

"Goodbye, Splash," he shouted.
"I'm going on holiday!"

The boat sailed on so far that Henry
couldn't see the ice and snow any more.

"Goodbye, Mummy Penguin," he whispered, and
he felt funny all over, and inside as well.

"Well, at least I'm not cold," Henry told himself firmly.
And he wasn't. As the boat sailed further and further,
the sun began to shine. It warmed Henry right down to his toes.

Suddenly Henry jumped with excitement.
There, just ahead of him, was his very own
tropical island! Henry dived into the
water and swam to the beach.

The island was full of palm trees and coconuts and pineapples.
Everything was bright and warm and colourful.
Henry was DELIGHTED!

But when he waddled up the beach, the sand wasn't soft and
smooth and slippery like the snow. It was hard and gritty and prickly.
"Never mind," said Henry. "It's nice and hot."

And it was. The sun beat down, until Henry began to feel very, very hot indeed.

Soon Henry was a very pink penguin.

"Never mind," he panted. "I'll go and have my supper. Those juicy pineapples will be delicious."

But the pineapples gave Henry tummy ache.

"Never mind," groaned Henry.
"Mummy Penguin will make it better."

But Mummy Penguin wasn't there.

That night, Henry sat on the beach
and looked up at the big white stars.
He missed the other baby penguins.
He missed Splash. He even missed the snow.

Most of
all, he missed
Mummy Penguin.

A cold little
tear ran down
his hot little face.

As he finally dropped off to
sleep, Henry made a decision.

The very next day, Henry waddled back over the
gritty, prickly sand and dived into the water.

He swam . . .

and swam . . .

and swam, until his feet ached.

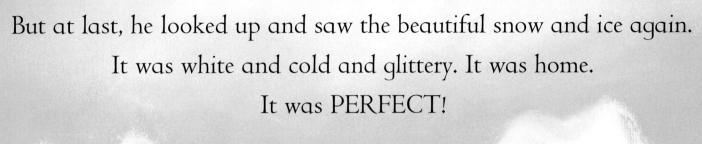

But at last, he looked up and saw the beautiful snow and ice again.
It was white and cold and glittery. It was home.
It was PERFECT!

"Hello snow!" Henry shouted, as he got closer.

"Hello penguins!" Henry shouted, as he got closer still.

"Hello Splash!" he shouted, as he jumped out of the icy water.

"Did you enjoy your holiday, Henry?" asked Splash.
"The very best bit about a holiday," smiled Henry,
"is definitely coming home again!"

From that day on, Henry rushed out to play in the snow every morning with his friends, and he was so busy sliding and diving that he forgot all about feeling cold . . .

And when he cuddled Mummy Penguin,
he felt warm all over, and inside as well.